THE VIRGINAL OF BIRDS

Also by M Sarki:

Zimble Zamble Zumble (limited edition, elimae books 2000) poetry

Zimble Zamble Zumble (trade edition, Author's Choice Press 2002) poetry

Little War Machine (Ravenna Press 2004) poetry

Mewl House (Rogue Literary Society 2005) poetry

Any Fucking Day (Rogue Literary Society 2009) poetry

Diary of the Modern God (Rogue Literary Society 2009)

Photographs: People, Places, and Nudes (Rogue Literary Society 2009)

Triple No. 2: No Entry (Ravenna Press 2012) poetry

Shorter Prose (Rogue Literary Society 2013)

Stamped Against the Night (Rogue Literary Society 2014)

Material to Destroy (Rogue Literary Society 2014)

No Entry (Rogue Literary Society 2014) poetry

Ailene Nou (Rogue Literary Society 2017)

The Mad Habit (Rogue Literary Society 2017)

THE VIRGINAL OF BIRDS

(Selected poems 1996-2012)
by M SARKI

COPYRIGHT

PUBLISHED BY THE
ROGUE LITERARY SOCIETY
https://rogueliterarysociety.com/
GAINESVILLE, FLORIDA

PRINTED IN THE USA

RLS009
ISBN-13: 979-8-218-20918-6

I. poetry II. Gordon Lish III. Beverly Lane
IV. eroticism V. infidelity VI. Florida
VII. relationships VIII. sexuality IX. art
X. memoir XI. song

ARTWORK AND DESIGN BY M SARKI

DEDICATION

For Beverly Lane and Gordon Lish

Table of Contents

*"The reading of a poem should be an experience. Its writing must be all the more so."*__Wallace Stevens from the book ***Opus Posthumous***

"I write to define myself—an act of self-creation—part of [the] process of becoming—In a dialogue with myself, with writers I admire living and dead, with ideal readers…" ___from ***Reborn: Journals and Notebooks, 1947-1963*** by Susan Sontag

"In an instant I had once again become conscious of the fact that one must not merely be constantly practising, having thoughts and quite simply practising with those thoughts, that one must also be constantly practising being able to express those thoughts at any time, for unexpressed thoughts are nothing…"__from **The Rest Is Slander: Five Stories** *by Thomas Bernhard*

Preface

The poems selected for this book were written between the years 1996 and 2012. All of my published collections prior to this book managed to not include any of these poems that follow. The impetus behind my choosing one poem over another has always been dictated by a certain feeling imposed while marshaling an entire composition into being. I believe form is everything, even in poetry. In addition there are also several other poems that were created during this same period that have yet to find their way into any collection of mine. Perhaps one day they too will have their place. But as I was deciding which poems to include in this book I was struck by how really hard and diligently I have worked since 1987 when I first began sending my scribblings to Gordon Lish for his approval. In the beginning it didn't go well for me. Ever since I can remember I had wanted first to be a novelist or short story writer. But Lish obviously wasn't buying it. Gordon remarked to me, well after I had proven my worth to him as a poet, that during those prior years he hadn't held much hope that I'd ever become a writer of any note. But I persisted in my writing, regularly mailing him pages, and never refusing to quit. After eight long years of accumulating a vast number of rejection slips from his magazine *The Quarterly,* Gordon finally invited me to study fiction-writing in his extensive private class held during the summer of 1995 on the campus of Indiana University in Bloomington. In his note to me he claimed that *Help was on the way!* And his class was life-changing. It was also a remarkable and surprising development that by the following year's class I had switched to writing poetry. At first Gordon dissuaded me and stated *poetry was for sissies.* But based on what Gordon was teaching, and also the poems he published in *The Quarterly,* I knew I could do it, and one day do it well. Especially the shorter ones. And it wasn't long at all before Gordon insisted I stick with my poetry and he began championing me.

Gordon Lish was not only my teacher, he became my friend. Early on he graciously informed my grown children that I was a *great American poet.* While dining one evening together he warmly expressed to my wife that *here sits a natural born poet.* Eventually I did begin to believe him and applied myself to becoming what I understood to be the strongest, hardest, and most interesting poet I could imagine. I studied the many words and constructions of Jack Gilbert, Wallace Stevens, Eugenio Montale, and Emily Dickinson, using their life's work as prime examples. Gordon also insisted I simply write poetry and not be concerned at all with self-aggrandizement. He promised the right people would one day eventually find me and come knocking on my door. And so I followed his austere advice, and for the last twenty-five years or so my focus has been specifically on my compositions and adding to the body of my work. And because my wife and I generally remain cloistered, few interested parties have actually come knocking.

Today I am sixty-nine years old. I haven't had a book of

poetry published since 2014. And the only way I'll ever be discovered for posterity is if that right person does find me. I have never networked. I have few friends. It is up to me to save myself which, when you come down to it, is what poetry is really all about. But my poems will do no good for others if they remain sitting in a drawer.

Gordon taught me that writers need to teach their readers how to read their work. And for me that means addressing the manner in which I come to my poems. If you are like me and hated poetry in school, and for the most part still do, that is a very hard task to demonstrate or explain. But if you are smart and bookish, and enjoy having a good time, then my poetry can definitely add to your fun. Words matter. And to be awed or surprised at the end of a poem, or left feeling a certain way that you never expected, or discovering how to perhaps look at things from a different point of view, then my poetry can be of some use.

It was a delight looking back on these seventy-two poems I selected for this book. It brought me home again to my enlightened time with Lish. Our personal and working relationship lasted almost twenty years, and for that I am eternally grateful. I forget exactly when he quit editing poems for me, but the last poem he actually approved for publication was *My Old Mungo* which was written in 2012. I had suffered a terrible accident in 2010 and though Lish claimed I was now writing some of my best poems, I had decided to quit writing poetry and focus instead on photography, prose, fiction, and memoir, as well as publishing my book reviews. I felt my work as a poet was finished and I did not want to repeat myself. Gordon was not pleased with my decision. He felt it was a mistake, and I did understand and appreciate all he had done for me in supporting and championing my prior work. I did send him a few poems in 2016 and he wrote back saying he was no longer able to look at them for me. Claimed his eyesight was sore and he was becoming blind. Age was definitely catching up with him so I reluctantly forgave him and left him in peace. But it was sad to lose that connection and his almost constant approval. So I again let my poetry go except for some experimental narrative pieces I composed for a project I titled *Stamped Against the Night*. But in December of 2022 I began a new poetry project, surprising myself once more, and these new poems do feel quite energetic and original. But patience demands I wait a few years before compiling these new poems into another book. Plus I enjoy observing how well they age. And if the poems are good now, they will be so later. So, I figure if I live long enough the poems I am writing today will also find their way into a manuscript. And it is my heartfelt wish that you will one day find them, and these, to your satisfaction.

—M Sarki

A Word from Gordon Lish
(Gordon's introduction to my work in the NY Tyrant)

"You see these bits by Sarki? You won't find bits like these exhibited under any name save his. This is because Sarki's triumph is to have succeeded in overcoming himself as poseur, the occupation consuming the best of us ordinarily, in order to release the poetry in universal occupancy. The bits that follow make sense to me. Is this a pose? Beats me. Like Sarki, I'm just doing what I might to have a terrific time too."

—Gordon Lish

THE POEMS
1996-2012

Long Beach

Oh! to fondle both
knobs on her radio

and to bite her teeth
into my apple.

Caught in the Broth, Gasping for Air

What mist of mustard
on this shoe?
Only photograph

he only trusted.
No wider truth
benign of tongue

sewn to his roof
and rafter.

Gianni's Testimone

What eye is holding
that candle back,
dyed by

the cross,
pushed from its
perse background?

Why fountains of
Rubelle's horses
brave this light.

And the face
of all glances,
shows.

Of Chippage and the Bud

Where do twisted feet,
with their haphazard
ventricles, go to

move on through
the knop? Is good
they plant them big

on Cold Spring Lane.

The Immovable Steel of Donegal

She did not,
could not,
fall in her wobble.

Such a proposal of
plastic, this mess.
What colossal infarction.

The element of
wagering.
Every canary.

And pindari wing.
The kites. The cardigan.
These bones.

The Steering Wheel

Each blind pinion
in the floor suggests
a warped cutter, or a

fractious shoal bent
on a forbidden example.
But say, now, no further

maculicolous departures
shall be granted. For
one must connect to being

sometimes the loneliest
perambulator on this planet.
And an eye for the sightless

and sore.

Near Sligo

Even with its landscapes
fully unresplendent,
no one apoplexes

at my party. Except
for an elderly woman
depositing receipts.

Her assets tied
to my cargo. And
smartly imparted.

So Berber, so tweed.

Museelmann! Preen Our Roses

Not coy but aloof inhumanity.
A tread nom de plume. An
insipid tear. Dolor overcome

by a difficulty unimaginable,
impossible to realize except
in its dying. A death so lonely

that even an outstretched hand
simply grazes it, disturbs the
bones, the chalking skeleton

broken-down but still alive
somehow to only what is left
of its viscosity.

Descending Argot of a Retired Hog Farmer

This is his chunky
pottage. His resolute
acumen for chowder.

A disembosomed
vulnerability producing
heroic evidence of an

old fallopian stroll.
The muscled being
of an excessive life.

The Sacred Text of Longing without End, Amen

We discriminate between
these strings and the range
of his response. The

movement proves
unearthly. Images,
aloft and obscure—nature

as anomaly. What grassland
he cuts through—what
whiskers! But know he

is the master behind
the official indifference.
His work still hangs

backstage. A ewer
best-braced for the
emergence of another

thought well made.

for Frank Lentricchia

Contours

My lies seem
not to crack.
They are pretty

as fossils. The
holes they make
are dark and

frightful. But
the surface
invites another

look. And the
ground beneath
them could

turn unstable.

Handsome Jim Anderson

His failure
is parquetteed
to reduce our

sympathy. A
disordered life
joined, here,

as sculpted
mass. Even
when viewed,

at the end of
the day, as a
book about a

duck in his
hands. Their
bronzed pages

curled by the
sun as in a
blinding effigy.

So many things
lovely and
dead, in this

reader's pose.

Friend

I feel it wiggling.
Sort of like an
invoice due.

But the specifics
avoid my body.
I am mindful

it must be you.

Young Woman in the Garden

An inkling
on her back
delighted

my curiosity.
A baroque
mark that

struck
me dumb.
So panic erupted.

And I dutifully
confessed to
anything.

Jesus

Hands ahead,
and you know
a carpenter's labor.

Calloused hearts
abhor when work
is difficult. Still,

it must have been
hard for you,
those handles.

That woodworker,
all smiles, and
causing you

to come in mere
minutes. But, wife,
you are back.

And I am feeling
myself again, my
prick making

its ingenious way
in fast.

Kim's Video

Our kids are
fraught by
the thought

of that
wrinkled
old prick

installed into
one of their
snappish pussies.

But it is
different
for us,

the aging—
cunts as favors,
and how

we farm.

Peeling Wax

You know
what it takes
to make

things right.
To maneuver
a sound into

something
geminous. A
locution in

which a vowel
gets out of bed.
Or one consonant

becomes
deliberate as
your fucking is.

Facing Winter's Bevy

There are feathers
drifting, piling into
the corner of my

room where last
May you loudly
did it to my wife.

I was in the bed
napping. I rolled
your way and

grabbed my cock.
Our eyes met.
And you smiled,

all the while your
fucking lasted,
until I, as a

ruined bird,
fell down on you,
and began

molting as a
cyclical person
would.

American Red Cross

Diving into
the deep part
of the freezing

Lake Huron,
my brother
looks good.

The rest of us
boys stand
there shivering.

Our naked toes
gripping the
icy deck as

Lenny explodes
from out of
the depths,

bobbing on
the plane,
all hell

spewing from
his lips.

When Grandpa Made His Blocks by Hand

There is little
smell of new
left on Helen.

Her shapeless
smock has
time-wafts in it.

Mournfully
she retreats from
him. Her

breasts falling
from the vine.

Michael Likes to Pretend

I dig for something
mysterious below me.
It is murky, but I am

audacious. I doubt
I will find it or be
happy if I do.

Disturbances are
imminent, time, you
know, is fugitive.

But I sit, mesmerized
in my stew. It won't
be long before I

will be no more.
And hard-pressed to
prove otherwise.

Square Hole

Why encourage
you to go in
to her? Isn't

she already
mine alone,
as in my

daily pleasure?
So what
counts most

to a person
such as myself,
the always

dissatisfied?
I say it is
unsayable.

Coupled
with a
pretentious

impulse
to meed.

The Scent of Robert Barbudo

They stalk the
meat of darters,
these shankers

often seen.
A filthy
swarm of

human flesh
in water to
their knees.

Salt Lick

She stands before
me pregnable
in her nakedness,

her strewn armor
on the floor,
but tossed with

nerve and
implication.
Translated, she

is a figure
of lowliness.
So I order her,

"Claim your pay."

And opening
this hunter's trap
I move to

free my leg.

We Were Losing Ground Before It Gave Way

Must have
been vanity,
these nude

photographs
spread about
his table.

She naked,
his strange
charge,

my wife
there, pleading.

Children of Our Murdered Chickens

The air still turns
in the June of
my tumbling.

A hard fall,
abrupt as my
crumbled bones.

My knee shattered
beyond the discovery
I was not dead.

Above me the
roof looked down.
Broken, my head

twisted in the
wet sand and
dirt she calls

her flower bed.
Long rides and
surgeries await

me. Feet clear
of the clutch
for the unknown

road ahead.

Before His Shoulder Made Ready

Somewhere a
word is missing
in the vast vocabulary

of the wounded sky.
The winged creatures
frantic in their telling.

Their cacophony of
discourse unrecognizable
to a mere mortal like

me. A morning
resplendent in its
pleading. An urgent

order to fly.

After Joe DiMaggio

The wind is whipping
at my pencil. Coloring
its delay in getting down

the hard marks of the day.
An old hammer stretched
naked on the cold floor.

That giant heap shrunk to
brittle bones and sagging
handles. The character

slipping away. Intent on
his riding. Refusing all
supplications patterned

on borrowing more time.

The Winter Kill of Chelsea Clinton

The kitchen was new
but not cheery. Done
in the mission of a man

who didn't love women.
Dark and dramatic as
the raging sea. Under-

currents dragging globules
off the wall, making
them start over. Riding

waves and crashing
at the break. Just as
the lady did rubbing her

wrist across the granite
counter top and wishing
for more rain.

Warm Air from a Knotted Stocking

She sleeps in that room,
or so he thinks. The
thick metal plates

clang on the busy
street until nothing
is at peace any

longer. That constant
motion of wheels
and rubber,

the insane cries from
another crazy on
the corner below

us. She with three
pillows wrapping
her head in

a vice of dead sound.
Unrelenting. A
prisoner to

the proof of a life
unmanageable.
And often

ridiculous.

Between Films

In one week I have watched
VHS biographies of William
Carlos Williams, Emily

Dickinson, James Stewart,
Henry Fonda, Brian Wilson,
and Jim Morrison. All

because I fell off my roof.
The luxury of free time
and how I spend it.

Marvelous stories, all of
them. How they lived,
and except for Wilson,

how they died. Though
he did too, a little bit.

Standing Pale and Dead in the Twilight

The rim of your bottle
looks like the sweat
band of my hat. A

treated cotton duck
with no feather in it.
A natural supplement

considered to
promote a healthy
heart once loved and

often forgiven
for the temper
of its skin.

He Draws Iron

There is no sound
before the big
break and

your old bones
shatter. Only
the rust in

the wind and
your pulsing matter.
You thumping as

the heal bores in.
A classic move
defined by a

veteran attacker.

The Bones Beneath Their Olive Skin

It was handsome,
this cut in the
play of the wave

of this rushing
boat swale. The
beef of the muffled

wind. A tight
knot on a loosening
intention known

only to him and
his companion.
Their last slip

into the molting
summer. That
soothing ache of

a drawn-out day.
And the mentioning
of no other.

The Shape of Unstable Ground

The storm ended as did the awful tax.
What lingered was a picture of
perfect sense even though it was

wet and smelled of a distant room,
long forgotten, sheltered, and with
its curtains drawn. Inside, the

last mouth was given to making
obscene sighs until the frame
of it heaved and pillowed what

remained of the wreckage of
his surroundings. It was a
strange brew that reminded

him of home for he dismissed
himself, gathered his broken things,
and made his way to the river

with its determined course and
specific method of meandering.

The Wind That Shunted Through the Gap

Curling, the torn
pages sank and
then bobbed

in the motion of
a saving device.
How the print

rode the waves
above the
bullate sand

and authored
its own fable,
tossed about

that sea of
thirst, the bunker
of a man

now drowning
off the coast
of California.

The Buttons Clasped Forever on Her Blouse

It is always the light that drapes
a corner of my world. And
ginger. The cultivated root

that can be recognized.
Everywhere is life and its
bidding. A telephone repaired

and catalog given. Or tanks
rolling over the scorched earth.
A muscling of engines and

the tightening of your throat.
A wide-screen format lost
to a box on the stage. The

muffling of tongues in a
tired parade of unforgiveables.
And some last chance for

salvation at the end of the day.

Where You Gathered Your Things

Yesterday I felt your note.
The manner in which it
flaked in my hand. Its

cragged edges scraping
into my skin. The
furrows making tiny

rivulets, forming a cast
of liquid in measures
invalid and notably

outlandish. Muscles
spread out on a shell.
And table settings.

The world as unseen
and without delight
except for a sick few

visiting.

The Horse Raised Its Nose and Nickered

There was a moment
in that hay when I felt
myself lagging.

Quietly I leaned into
you and let myself
go. Those fingers;

strangers bent on
discovery. Looking
back, it was a rather

shameful act. A
bad move. And
I am sorry

those buggers hadn't
a clue for what to
do in order to

make you happy.

And the Bolt Ran Forever on That Wind

There is a tax associated
to relaxed summer days
and their idle tallying. The

end weight of string in
the distance of one glorious
day. That beady measure

of hope caught in the
blink of a reckoning. But
all else is work and suffering,

our daily grumblings that
divide each day.

When Disease Destroyed the Indian

The cliff sculpture
fell. Its slivers and
chunks now dust

on the former land-
scape. Its surface
interrupted by this

crumbling affair
that man had made
in his image. A

pile of debris.
Unstructured form.
The careful look

of decay.

She Seemed a Circus Departing in Hats

Tidy lines are lost
on the canvas.
Fair piles and torturous

assaults draw the
bangled eye of this
man. An ear for

her in the bed a
room over, rustled
like a steer from his

voltaire. A wamble
for the reference
he steps into.

The maze of her
genitals. Flesh
laundered by rain.

The audience
and those breasts,
them feeding on

her, mindful of
the haste in which
she eventually

will flee.

The Peregrine Bones of a Prophet

There are movements
before the great
dance commences.

A swelling of sway
and collar braced
against the overcast

sky. The flesh of
a green leaf yellowing.
Then, somewhat

horrifying, the repugnant
straits of displaced air
and rolling rubber.

An interruption meant
for me. The chance

to change my mind.

The Dark Head of Weather

Even after my hair settles
and my limb breaks in two
she cares enough to sleep

near me peacefully, her chin
squeezed between two pillows
made from lamb's wool. I

cup one breast and count my
blessings quietly, protective
of my need, always,

for more.

Instead of Calling for the Landlord

Two feet of snow
and the heat of a
thousand candles.

Not enough for
indigent boys to
remain in the

city springs of
Colorado. Beer
and LSD.

Sticky girls and
shovels heaped
with tomorrow.

Finding oil in
our maddening
dash away

and settling
instead for a
trip gorging

itself on trouble.

Eating the Dead From Out of Their Clothes

I like fish smell
and cedar. The
rest before

a sawmill plank.
A fine explosion
before dinner.

What else could
this wretched boy
make but trout

and potatoes?
Feasting as a king.
And all before it

comes too late.

Ray Carver

She quickly wrapped a leg
around the man in the elevator.
Threw him down on all fours

and arm-locked his neck until
he cried uncle. He remembered
her underwear. Ruffled. And

the stain on her front door.

The Serious Debt

The sampling she made
seemed innocent enough.
Her plants gave off a
strange odor. Somewhere
another cloud lifted to
brighten the sky. But the
couple continued to excuse
their existence until a ladder
fell, seriously breaking the
ground below them.

In Bloomington

I went to market raw as fish and spent
my time instead on an Underwood.
There, typing notes left inside my head
after another night of sleeping alone,
miles distant from my wife. The hippie
chick exquisite with her unchained
breasts swinging as shafts do light
under a welcome sign. But I remained,
as the shoes did, outside his motel door,
lined attentively in pairs, wondering
what those two could be doing alone in
there, maybe in that bed, in another
room other than my own.

Long After the Burial

She with her
panties hanging
caught around

her knees. Me,
with the undertaker
forming his opinion

as to why she
seems so pleased.

The Cripple of Sixth Avenue

He spun fast and held to the
hawthorn branch, beseeching
his son to hurry to his labor.
One pirouette and the fat
man's dance. Deaf ears and
the awful trembling. His
wife frantic in the street, the
motion of her hands screaming
for their son to gather this
husband going down. The
window glass on the corner
and the slant of the sidewalk
his big mistake. The urgent
planting of their feet and all
this mustering.

Water Coming Down from West Virginia

Where the sea lumps folded our
forgiveness into pies of sorts,
we fell down. It was there we

made our day. And traveled
after as in road trips meandering
upstream. Capturing trout

among the war paint and faces.
None clouded so severely as our
own, the gray cast as solemn as

the corn stalks drying against
these fields of hay.

An Old Score

Richard Hugo trims my hair
and winces at the container of
Asian noodles steaming in his

neighbor's barbering contraption.
I learn so much from people here.
The handling of these shears and

the confidence gained in trusting
good tools. The trade seems
remarkable for all its undoing.

The way legends are made.
The cut that seems fair.

Temperatures Below Twenty

No explanation for his cold stare on
these hard streets of heaven. After
fifty years I doubt he still recognizes

me. I am, however, confused by all
this hatred here. Must mention the
gold pavers gleaming on streets so

close to the sun. And my father now,
his back against a pillar, whistling some
tune he must have learned in the Navy.

Shaping a World

Glass looks good on a
soft-waxed floor. The
harboring of textures.

An envelope remains.
But what becomes of
a buggered life built,

I jest, for solitude?
Ramblings from a
furtive mind, stacking

all these dishes on
their hot-lipped stove.

The Rule of My Jungle

The walls are fast with
photographs of summer.
Her nude body cast

against the pine landscape
the sun makes harsh and
penetrating. Her form

stately on the forest path.
Her bush a meadow I
would gladly walk into.

The Extent of Our Chances

I tied a leader to the belt
of an old crow and whistled
a tune I learned of candied

apples. There we bored
her flesh and ground the crisp
fruit to slow the traffic

around here. The young
birds still flew, diving deep
to break our tethers.

Wives in their best suits
gathered to welcome our
hand in making life possible

with us so clearly out of
the way.

After the Little Big Horn

Their laughter grew so loud
the cattle stirred. Awake in
my boots, I patted the crest

of my pony, waiting for
daybreak and a fresh cup
of coffee. Napped until

the sun burned my hair and
felt that beast behind no
breeze coming for me.

Grabbed my hat and ran
for the nearest saloon,
thinking of you and how

we used to be happy.
Before the cattle, cowboys,
coffee, and this full moon.

Toothpaste, Tape, and a New Cooler

She was fond of doors
and the box of candles
hidden behind his linen

curtain. Photographs
were made. Clothes
strewn on oak floors

the lady had not cleaned
since Sunday. She was
married, but not happily.

He was a missionary.
And played to the curious
manner in which she prayed,

beneath his robe, to ghosts,
in particular.

Fumbling with Removing His Pants

In case you
had not
noticed this

white lock
of hair
let us

place it
on this
pretty dish

where the
moon can
reach it.

The Future of Our Forests

The trees have become
carnivorous and ugly. No
longer limbed with fronds

of needled leaves but
armed instead with
fiddleheads and hands

rough off the plow. Now
the beasts make claim on
their hunger. They demand

more food. My last
remembered comfort a
year ago seated in my cabin's

stuffed chair gazing out
my window. The softness
everywhere, the outdoors

inviting. Now all these
animals are forgetting my
name. My stardom at

once fleeting and delusional.

The Fork

She says there is nothing
left in the filthy cupboard
now that you have allowed

the rest of them to ravage
her. That you actually
expected a different result

ludicrous, and for that matter,
beyond fucking belief. She
means she has been had by

so many of your so-called
friends that fucking has
become a business for her

and she would like to be paid.
And she adds, in something
more than change.

Thinking on the Cascade

Marks scribed on the widened
slab indicate futility. A somewhat
grave and profane scribbling to
determine the meaning of their
story. A confused hashing of
unlawful signatures splayed on
this plain of concrete mist, its
smell distinctive by its sour tip
to bad odor. The exhaustive
sweat after all their fucking.
A generation of raw and virgin
steel. The moment involved
in recognizing aliens from
another planet.

For the Love of Women

The fog was lifting
off the furnace
near this precipice.

Never had the
couple witnessed
a haze so benevolent

or a fire of such haste.
With remarkable
courage she took her

final steps, laughed
heartily, and plunged.
The man paused to

examine his mind,
and furthermore,
to exist for a moment

among the falling ash.

The Theater of Cruelty

She gestured for
the roughest boy
to move in closer

as she undid the
buttons on her
blouse. Remarkable

how those hands
made her flesh
tingle after long

hours spent fumbling
with melting wax
cakes she poured

into forms to make
mannequins. An
enterprise that

allowed her to
keep abreast of her
brawny prisoner.

A Jolly Climb to the Peak Ends

Willie Graham
and James McEllison.
John J. Collins

and Patrick Fogarty.
J. B. Haws and
Oscar Buchart.

M. J. Norton
and William Lydon.
Melvina S. Goldbach

and yes, Mary
Hesson McGue.

Poor Dirt Road

Her gift of stew mattered
to the old gentleman. The
blend of root vegetables

made a pleasant picture
and lifted his thoughts
above what he called

the cumulus. It rarely
came that she would stay,
but the moment of his

abrupt return, fresh
from his far-off thinking,
he would look for her

from across the room,
always hoping for even a
glimpse of one of her trifles.

After Reading Four Pages of Dalí

What ails the seeker
as restitution lingers
and remains

unreachable? The
pillow of prosperity
rising as a hot air

balloon aloft in the
western sky.
The tangling of

guide lines
becoming a
masterpiece

of design upon
the crumbling earth.
And the screaming

hoards of onlookers
resembling cattle
led willfully

to their slaughter.

When She No Longer Feels Ill

Rains made the vibrant
shag of ground cover
happy. Straddling

the fallen tree, her
naked bottom shined
with the yolk of

fresh spring water.
Her nipples erect
to both my stare

and the adjustments
I made to the settings
on my camera. I

rushed for the one
chance to capture
the arch of her back,

her shuddering copy
in the nervous branches
surrounding her

in front of the darkened
box recording our
little masterpiece.

Long Before Their End is Near

Further the couple
rambled into the
unfamiliar. Their

riches, of course,
mounting as
experience shared

and collaborated.
Conquests making
slaves of each other.

And a finger on the
meaning of what matters.

When Your Scutcher Met This Finn

The meter jammed
and I was either
fortunate or forlorn.

A gulf I am
accustomed to. A
reckless life within

walking distance
of home. And the
measured gait of

a man she still
deems impossible.

My Old Mungo

Careful with that
shovel near the
dew-laden branch.

Pound out the
spirits left under-
neath your hat.

The flame carried
diligently from
youth onto the

grave. A retention
of your credence
long ago.

Afterword

"It is not every day that the world arranges itself in a poem." __Wallace Stevens from the book ***Opus Posthumous***

*"From a certain point onward there is no longer any turning back. This is the point that must be reached."*__Franz Kafka

*"Why consider as a flaw the act of yielding, the fact that we are susceptible to others? Feelings, sensations, and desires can lie dormant until brought into being by those around us. We need to be able to allow this, too; we need not to fight so hard against our own porousness, our own malleability…Sometimes, the deepest pleasure is in letting someone in…Working out what we want is a life's work, and it has to be done over and over and over. The joy may lie in it never being done."*__from ***Tomorrow Sex Will Be Good Again: Women and Desire in the Age of Consent*** by Katherine Angel

About the Author

For the last several years M Sarki has maintained a literary blog called *The Rogue Literary Society* which can be found at https://rogueliterarysociety.com/ where he publishes his critical views on subjects and books read, photographs and nude art collaborations with his wife, as well as periodical attempts at creating poetic artifacts. Since 2000 Sarki has produced four collections of poetry and four books of prose. M Sarki has also written, directed, and produced four short art films titled *Gnoman's Bois de Rose*, *Biscuits and Striola*, *The Tools of Migrant Hunters*, *My Father's Kitchen,* and he is the author of the feature film screenplay, *Alphonso Bow.*

www.ingramcontent.com/pod-product-compliance
Lightning Source LLC
LaVergne TN
LVHW010629100826
845148LV00014B/3174

9798218209186